Snow...

Written by Alison Milford

Illustrated by Sally Newton

FULL FLIGHT

Titles in Full Flight 4

Badger Publishing Limited
15 Wedgwood Gate, Pin Green Industrial Estate,
Stevenage, Hertfordshire SG1 4SU
Telephone: 01438 356907. Fax: 01438 747015
www.badger-publishing.co.uk
enquiries@badger-publishing.co.uk

Snowboard Adventure ISBN 1 84691 028 5
                    ISBN 978-1-84691-028-9

Series Editor: Jonny Zucker
Publisher: David Jamieson
Commissioning Editor: Carrie Lewis
Editor: Paul Martin
Design: Fiona Grant
Illustration: Sally Newton

Snowboard Adventure

Contents

The Olympic Dream

"Look at Martha Malone go! The snow's flying off her board as she rides at high speed down the freestyle run. Just listen to the crowd cheering snowboarding's brightest new star!"

Martha! Martha!

"Martha! Did you hear me?"

Martha looked at her mum.
"Sorry, what did you say?" asked Martha dreamily.

"I've-ordered-us-hot-chocolate!" said Martha's mum slowly.

"Thanks mum!"

Martha stared happily out of the café window at the snow-covered mountains. She was finally here!

"Two hot chocolates, ladies," smiled a waiter, holding a tray of steaming mugs.

A man, whose face was half hidden by a scarf, pushed past, knocking the tray as he went.

"Hey! Be careful! These drinks are hot!" shouted the waiter.

The man coughed loudly and rushed out of the door.

"How rude!" said Martha's mum crossly. "He didn't even say sorry."

"I expect he's rushing off to buy the last few tickets for tomorrow's Snowboard Freestyle competition," smiled the waiter.

"Martha is going in that," said Martha's mum proudly. "She is a brilliant snowboarder."

Martha felt herself go red as the waiter looked at her with interest.

"I've heard that the winner will get lots of prize money," said the waiter.

Martha nodded. "But what I really want is the other prize – a place on the next Olympic snowboard team."

The waiter pointed at a tall girl walking past the window with her snowboard. "First you've got to beat last year's freestyle winner, Anna Anderson. I hear she doesn't like to lose."

Grabbing her jacket and snowboard, Martha headed quickly for the door.

"Great, I love a challenge," she called excitedly. "See you later!"

Anna v Martha

Martha looked down the steep run that had been set up for the freestyle competition. Other snowboarders were busy practising their freestyle tricks and air jumps on the bumpy slope.

"Too hard for you?" asked a voice behind her.

Martha swung round and looked straight into the face of Anna Anderson. "I was just checking out the line of the slope before I ride it," replied Martha.

Anna scowled. She looked down at Martha's blue snowboarding boots. "Why have you got radar signal stickers on your boots?" she smirked.

"You only need those if you get into trouble out on the open slopes."

"I think they look really cool," grinned Martha, "and it's better to be safe than sorry."

Anna laughed nastily. "I agree. You should drop out of the competition before you get hurt!"

Martha laughed back. She was not going to let Anna Anderson upset her. "Don't worry about me," said Martha. "I'm a great snowboarder and I intend to win!"

Anna glared angrily at Martha. "You don't stand a chance. The prize money and the Olympic place will be mine and nothing will stop me. Nothing!"

Pushing Martha out of the way, Anna tipped the nose of her snowboard over the edge of the run and made sharp turns into the hard snow.

A loud cough stopped Martha from following. A man, wearing dark ski goggles, stood close by. It was the same man that had pushed by them in the café.

"Can I help you?" called out Martha.

Without a word, the man shoved a notebook into his rucksack, and skied quickly away.

Martha was puzzled. What was he doing up here?

Go! Martha

In the changing room, Martha nervously put her number vest over her jacket. She was to be the third snowboarder down the run.

Martha took a deep breath and ran through her freestyle tricks and moves in her head.

A judge with a clipboard walked in. "Please clip your bindings onto your boots and line up outside. The competition is about to start."

Outside, Martha could hear the cheer of the crowds at the bottom of the run.

The first girl moved to the run's edge and waited for the starting bell to ring.

Ding Ding Ding!

The snowboarder quickly found a good line to ride down the slope. Suddenly her board went in too deep round a corner and she fell into the hard snow.

Ding Ding Ding!

The second snowboarder slid her snowboard onto the run.

Martha felt worried. Something was wrong but she didn't know what.

"Five seconds to go, Miss Malone," said the starting judge.

Martha stepped onto her snowboard and bent her knees.

Suddenly, a loud scream filled the air. "Stop thief! Somebody help! The prize money has been stolen!"

Martha looked up and saw a figure with a rucksack quickly snowboard across to the open slopes of the mountain.

Ding Ding Ding!

"Go, Miss Malone!" called out the judge.

Martha looked around her. Why was nobody moving? If the thief got away, the competition could be called off and her hopes for the Olympics ruined.

"I thought she would be too scared," laughed Anna.

"Miss Malone, will you please jump off!" shouted the judge.

Martha unclipped ber boots and ran off the course. Clipping her boots back into the bindings, she followed the marks of the thief's snowboard.

She had to stop the thief!

Stop That Thief

The slope was steep and bumpy. Martha rode her snowboard quickly across the hard snow.

Suddenly the thief rode up to the top of a snow ridge, half turned in the air and came down again. The thief waved cheekily at Martha.

"That was very good," said Martha to herself. "But I'm better!"

With knees bent, Martha pushed her snowboard over the edge of the ridge. High up in the air she did a full spin. She carved her snowboard from side to side, getting faster as she went. The thief swerved round a large rock.

"Oh no! I can't stop," gasped Martha. "I'm going to have to jump over the rock!"

Tucking her arms under her knees, Martha did a full flip in the air and landed right in front of the thief.

Taken by surprise, the thief swerved past her.

"Stop!" screamed Martha. "Not that way!"

Martha stared in horror as the thief fell over the edge of the mountain. Martha ran to the edge. Looking down she saw that the thief had landed on a ledge.

In pain the thief took off the dark goggles.

Martha gasped in shock. "You!"

"Help me! I think I've broken my leg!" begged the thief. It was the waiter who had brought their hot chocolate the day before.

Martha looked down at his twisted, bloodied leg and knew he was right. "Take a deep breath," said Martha calmly, "and try to stay still."

"You'd better go and get help. I don't want to be stuck here all night!" moaned the waiter.

"You'll be fine," said Martha. "The radar stickers on my boots will let the mountain rescue team know where we are. They should be here any minute."

Martha was puzzled. "Why did you steal the prize money?"

The waiter sighed deeply. "Once I was the top Half Pipe snowboarding champion. I used to perform amazing tricks off the walls of the pipe."

Martha stared at the waiter in shock. "You're John Burns!" she exclaimed. "I heard that you were caught cheating."

The waiter scowled nastily. "Thanks to those stupid competition judges I've been banned from competing ever again. I took the prize money because they ruined my life!"

"You're the one who ruined it," Martha retorted.

A loud chug-chug sound filled the sky as a mountain rescue helicopter headed straight towards them.

Martha watched as mountain rescue pulled the waiter and the rucksack up into the helicopter.

"Do you want a lift back?" shouted down the rescuer.

"What happened to the competition?" asked Martha.

"It still went ahead," shouted back the man.

"In that case, I'll snowboard back down," said Martha glumly.

All alone, Martha looked at the dazzling white snow and the clear blue sky above her. She smiled. She may have lost the competition but she just had one of the most thrilling rides of her life.

Breathing in the icy, cold air, Martha rode side to side through the trees back to the ski resort.

The Prize

Martha didn't want to be at the prize giving. She felt tired and sad, but her mum told her that she must go.

The crowd clapped as the local mayor walked onto a platform with the prize money.

"Please welcome this year's freestyle champion – Anna Anderson," he said loudly.

Anna strolled onto the platform, took the money and smirked at Martha.

"That girl should never have won," said her mum angrily. "Her jumps were far too easy and her tricks were very boring."

"Don't worry, mum," smiled Martha weakly. "Let's go and get a hot chocolate."

As they walked away, Martha heard a loud cough. It was the man who had bumped their hot chocolate in the café – and he was coming straight towards Martha!

"Who are you?" she demanded.

"My name is Dan Lamb. I'm here to choose a snowboarder for the Olympic team," he explained.

"Anna Anderson is over there!" snapped Martha crossly as she pointed over to the platform.

"I'm not interested in Anna," grinned the man. "In the last two days I've been trying to watch you in secret." The man started to cough.

"I think your cough gave you away," laughed Martha.

The man nodded. "Your snowboarding skills are fantastic. The place on the Olympic team is yours, if you want it."

Martha was stunned. "Thank you. I won't let you down. I promise!"

"I also overheard the mayor say that you will get a large reward for getting the prize money back," smiled the man.

"I think it's time to celebrate," grinned Martha's mum.

"First, I want to try out a jump I've just learnt," said Martha excitedly.

"Haven't you had enough snowboarding for one day?" said her mum.

"You know me!" laughed Martha. "I just love a challenge!"